This Walker book belongs to :

_____

_____

_____

Not so long ago, a tooth fairy
took a call on her mobile.
"April Underhill here."
With one finger in her ear against
the traffic noise, she listened.
"You're his grandma?
No, my sister Esme and I
don't do tooth visits yet.
Our mum and dad always…
You want US?
We shall be there.
I PROMISE."

For Lola, Sadie and Poppy

First published 2010 by Walker Books Ltd
87 Vauxhall Walk, London SE11 5HJ

This edition published 2012

10 9 8 7 6 5 4 3 2 1

The right of Bob Graham to be identified as author/illustrator
of this work has been asserted by him in accordance with the
Copyright, Designs and Patents Act 1988

This book has been typeset in Poliphilus and Blado MT.

Printed in China

British Library Cataloguing in Publication Data:
a catalogue record for this book is available from the British Library

ISBN 978-1-4063-3960-4

www.walker.co.uk

April Underhill, Tooth Fairy

Bob Graham

The North
M 42 ↑

WALKER BOOKS
AND SUBSIDIARIES
LONDON · BOSTON · SYDNEY · AUCKLAND

April Underhill opened the door.
A draught slipped through behind her and Esme,
making the teeth on the rafters chatter and chime.
John Underhill started to speak. "April…"

"Don't say anything, Daddy," April said. "We're collecting a boy's tooth tonight, and I have to write this down…"

Daniel
Dangerfield
3 Cornflower
Terrace
Parkville Milk
Tooth front
Dog, no Cat
Tonihgt

"TONIGHT? April, you're only seven," said her dad. "And three quarters," April added. "I promised."

"I'm going too," said Esme.

"You and Esme? A tooth in Parkville?" said their mum, Fay.
"Darlings, you're far too young."

"You went by yourself when you were six, Mummy," said Esme.
She balanced a bubble on the end of her finger, till it popped.
"Same age as me – and April's even older."

"Well that was long ago," said Mum. "Before the motorway came.

Foxes still chased hares on the hill and things were different back then."

"Well, some things haven't changed, Mummy…"
Esme took a sip of her dandelion soup.
"Children still lose their first teeth," April said,
"and ducklings still have to take their first swim."

Their parents looked at them, startled.
"OK," said Dad. "You can both go – but
take great care of your little sister, April."

"Yes!"

"This is important, April," said Dad.
"To Daniel you are a … a … spirit of the air.
You are magic. He must never see you."

"Magic? ME?" said April.

Mum found a string bag.
"For the coin going out – and
the tooth coming back," she said.

"And send me a text if you need to," she added.

Then
they
lifted off
into the night.

The North
M42 ↑

and shook them …

pushed them and pulled them.

The wind took them …

It shivered down Esme's wings …

and rippled through the feathers of a passing owl.
"There's Cornflower Terrace!" shouted April.
They dropped down through the dark …

… right onto the doorstep of Daniel's house.
They peered underneath.

April swallowed. "Hold down my wings, Esme. I'll go first."

Esme crawled in after her …

... to the other side. "Where will his room be?" she whispered.

"Up there, I think," replied April.
"Let's follow the toys."

"This must be him," whispered April.
   She pulled the note from her pocket.
"We're at number three, Cornflower Terrace.
   There's a dog, but no cat…"
"And THERE'S THE TOOTH!"
   Esme shivered with excitement.

"But, oh dear!
He's put it in water,"
said April.

She made a decision. "I can swim. I'll get it."

She squeezed her eyes shut and,
in a cloud of bubbles, went for the bottom.
"I've got it, Esme! I've got it!"

"Shhh!" hissed Esme …

as Daniel Dangerfield stirred …

and woke!

April flew and Esme followed her. Together they pulled
Daniel's eyes shut, like the blinds over windows.
For a long time, they dared not breathe.

"He's asleep again," April whispered.
"But he SAW us," Esme whispered back.

"I'll text Mummy,"
said April.

"Whisper what?"
Esme asked, as
they read her reply.

"What Daddy told us.
That we're spirits."

"You do it, April,"
said Esme.
"Me? I'm soaking."

But she leaned into the dark and whispered,
"We're spirits of the air, Daniel. You dreamed us.
You did not see us."

"Goodbye, Daniel Dangerfield!"
They picked up the tooth and
flew down the hall.

"April, wait!" called Esme.

"It's the sweetest sight …

I think it's the grandma."

April waded waist-deep in Grandma's hair, then kissed her on the nose. "We did it, Grandma. Our very first tooth," she whispered. "No, Esme, we don't take those. We have to go."

They collected their coats,
buttoned them tight
and slipped
under the door.

Daniel's front tooth swung
in its bag, as they cleared
the chimney and headed
for home.

The wind tumbled them
high over the city,
up the motorway
and set them down ...

at their own front door.
Mum and Dad hugged
them till their wings
crackled.

"Here's the tooth, Daddy,
wrapped in my wet vest."
"You dived for it?" asked Fay.

"Like a duckling in water,"
murmured John Underhill
proudly.

The girls drank hot elderberry juice,
and then were hugged some more.

Mum hung Daniel's tooth from the rafters.
"On Saturday, we'll take it to the Fairy Craft Market
for everyone to see," Dad promised.

The sun rose and a blackbird sang outside the window,
louder than the distant traffic. As April and Esme fell asleep …

Daniel Dangerfield woke to find a coin gleaming by his bedside.
A new tooth was already growing. What dreams he'd had!

*Out on the motorway,
a wild hare scampered across
six lanes of traffic,
 past an old stump,
  a tiny house,
and up to its time-worn
tracks on the hill.
Nose twitching, it looked over
its shoulder for foxes,
then far out to the horizon...*

BOB GRAHAM

Bob Graham is one of Australia's finest author-illustrators.
Winner of the Kate Greenaway Medal, Smarties Book Prize and CBCA
Picture Book of the Year, his stories are renowned for celebrating the magic
of everydayness. Bob says, *"I'd like reading my books to be a little like opening
a family photo album, glimpsing small moments captured from daily lives."*

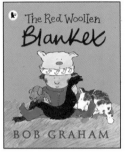

ISBN 978-1-4063-1649-0

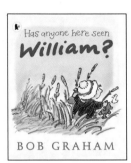

ISBN 978-1-4063-1613-1

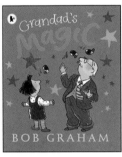

ISBN 978-1-4063-1647-6

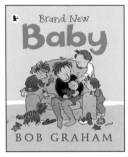

ISBN 978-1-4063-1640-7

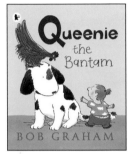

ISBN 978-1-4063-1648-3

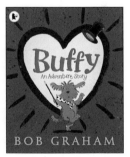

ISBN 978-1-4063-1650-6

ISBN 978-0-7445-9827-8

ISBN 978-1-4063-0851-8

ISBN 978-1-84428-482-5

ISBN 978-1-4063-0132-8

ISBN 978-1-4063-0686-6

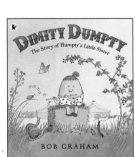

ISBN 978-1-4063-1901-9

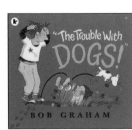

ISBN 978-1-4063-2601-7

ISBN 978-1-4063-2549-2

ISBN 978-1-4063-3419-7

Available from all good booksellers

www.walker.co.uk